This is Lionel.
Lionel loves clothes.

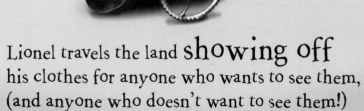

Lionel travels the land **showing off** his clothes for anyone who wants to see them, (and anyone who doesn't want to see them!)

1

He can pedal his Fashion Wagon and set up his fashion show anywhere he likes. He rolls out the special catwalk and parades up and down, modelling his wonderful collection of garments.

He has spotty shirts and stripy trousers, fancy hats and pointy shoes, tight fitting trouser suits and oh-so-trendy dresses, in fact any garment you can think of – he just loves them all.

And he gets **so cross** when people don't like what he's wearing!

3

He likes to sport this delightful lounge jacket...

...with these carefully selected pantaloons.

Or a spotty pinafore over a leopard-skin leotard...

...with matching beret and wellies....

4

This **safari** jacket...

...goes very well with this **tutu**...

...and these **flared** trousers...

...with **stiletto** heels.
(Lionel thinks).

Here, some **frilly** bloomers with a pirate's tunic, set off very nicely with a **bowler** hat and **sandals**.

Cummerbunds, cravats, culottes or spats – everyday something different...

And he is **always** on the lookout for a new piece of clothing to add to his collection…

I wonder where he is pedalling the Fashion Wagon to today?

Wherever it is,
I hope he will find an
appreciative audience!

Perhaps he will see
some new clothes
to add to his collection?

He has rolled out his catwalk and prepared himself for his first display.

And someone's coming!

Who is it...?

It's Mrs. Witch! Will she like what he's wearing?

8

Mrs. Witch has stopped dead in her tracks!

"What on Earth does he think he looks like?" she is muttering to herself.

Lionel is fascinated by her hat. So different! So stylish!

He's telling Mrs. Witch he wants to swap it for his 'Fuchsia' hat.

9

"Not on your Nelly!" screeches Mrs. Witch.
Her Grandmother made it for her, out of some rare spider's
cobwebs, and you just can't get them any more.

"How ridiculous ~
that tutu looks
awful with that
hat!" she shouts, as
she walks away with
her nose in the air.

Lionel is **growling** under his breath... But listen... I can hear footsteps. It's Mr. Watt!

He's left his shed to fetch some more tools.

Quick! Change your clothes Lionel!

11

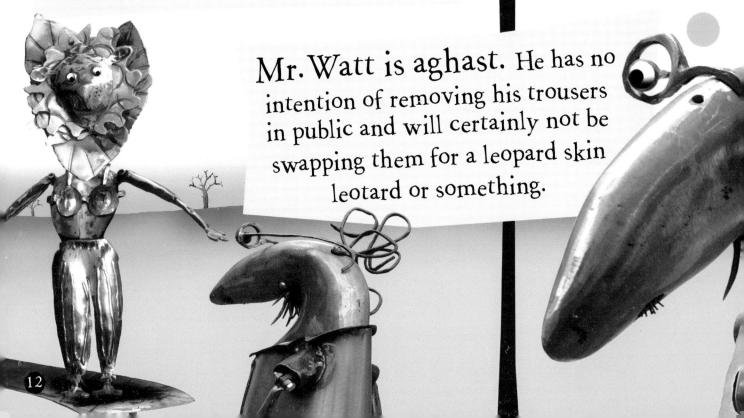

Lionel is very taken with Mr. Watt's trousers and tells Mr. Watt to kindly remove them so he can try them on.

Mr. Watt is aghast. He has no intention of removing his trousers in public and will certainly not be swapping them for a leopard skin leotard or something.

12

Lionel looks very cross
as Mr. Watt beats
a hasty retreat.

13

Now Lionel can hear
a trundling noise.
It's Posh Dog rolling
down the road!

Lionel is
immediately
eyeing up Posh
Dog's bow~tie
and Posh Dog is
feeling decidedly
uncomfortable...

14

...his Great Great Grandmother won it in a stick throwing competition 100 years ago, and no way is Posh Dog going to part with it.

Posh Dog mumbles something about needing to see a dog about a man, and quickly rolls away.

15

Juggling Jack Russell has come round the bend and dropped all of his juggling bones in surprise.

He took one look at Lionel's mini skirt and couldn't help blurting out

"What HAS that lion got on?" before quickly picking up his bones and running away.

Lionel fumed, but wasn't too bothered because Juggling Jack Russell wasn't wearing anything that Lionel liked either (in fact Juggling Jack Russell wasn't wearing anything at all!)

Next up it's
the Parson!

"Oh I say!"
says Lionel when
he sees the
Parson's cassock
and dog collar.

"Oh I say!" says the
Parson, who can't believe
anyone would think it was
OK to wear a hat like that
with socks that colour.

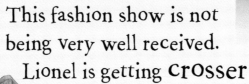

This fashion show is not
being very well received.
Lionel is getting **crosser**
and **crosser** by
the minute.

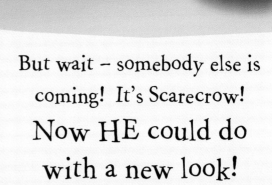

But wait – somebody else is
coming! It's Scarecrow!
Now HE could do
with a new look!

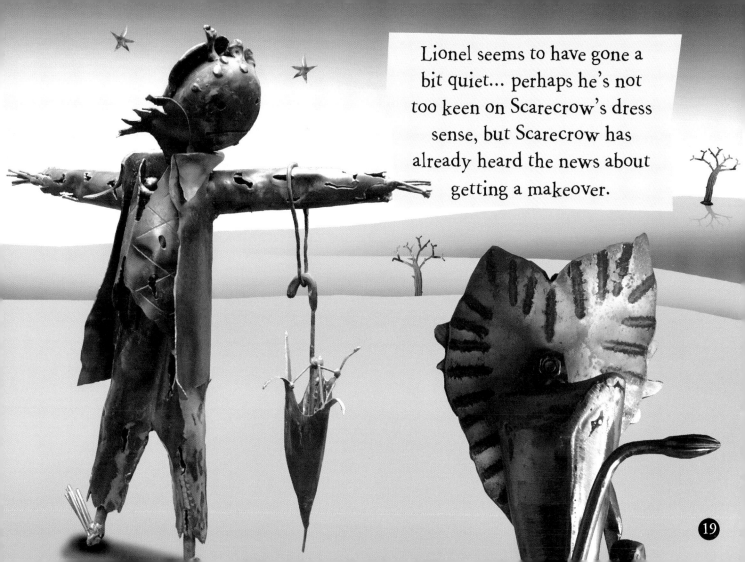

Lionel seems to have gone a bit quiet... perhaps he's not too keen on Scarecrow's dress sense, but Scarecrow has already heard the news about getting a makeover.

Lionel is trying to quickly roll up his catwalk, but too late! Scarecrow is already trying on his pirate's tunic! And his leotard! And his bowler hat!

Scarecrow is looking pretty smart – even Lionel thinks so!

In fact so much so, that Lionel is offering Scarecrow a mirror to look at himself in.

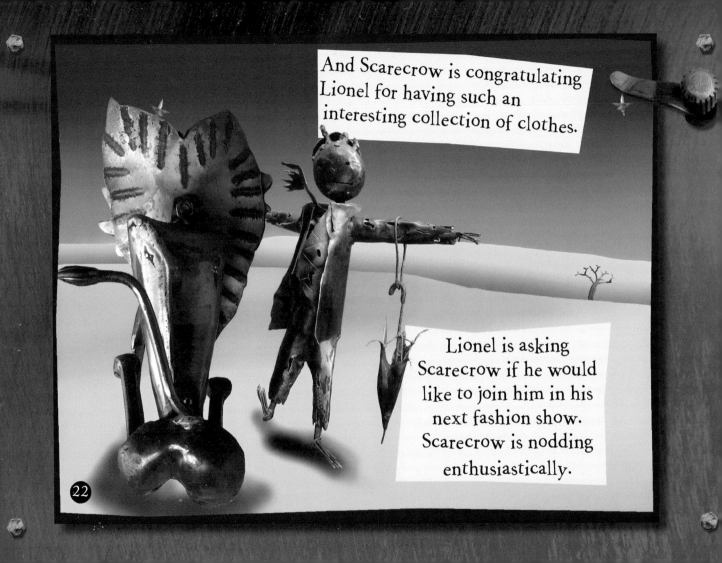

And Scarecrow is congratulating Lionel for having such an interesting collection of clothes.

Lionel is asking Scarecrow if he would like to join him in his next fashion show. Scarecrow is nodding enthusiastically.

22

Scarecrow has helped Lionel roll up the catwalk and has offered to pedal the Fashion Wagon. Lionel is VERY happy – not very cross at all!

I think they're going to get along together very well!

23

All books available on iPad & iPhone,
and some as printed versions! Check out
and follow the links on mrwatt.biz today!

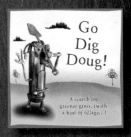

Go Dig Doug!

A search for greener grass, (with a hint of tillage...)

Posh~Dog and his light relief.

A wee tale of courtesy and satisfaction...

The Leaf Lady Cometh

by Jon Mills

Feo (for short)

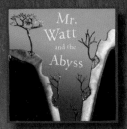

Mr. Watt and the Abyss

Mr. Watt & Iron Pig:

a tale of manufacturing, marketing and the environment!

Mrs. Choir and her concerted effort:

a tale of discord and comeuppance!

by Jon Mills